JACK
IN THE
GREEN

JACK
IN THE
GREEN

CHARLES DE LINT

Illustrated by Charles Vess

Subterranean Press 2014

First Edition

ISBN
978-1-59606-641-0

Subterranean Press
PO Box 190106
Burton, MI 48519

subterraneanpress.com

IT'S NOT THE AUDACITY of the invasion that shocks Maria so much as that she recognizes one of the robbers: Luz Chaidez. Maria hasn't thought of her in years.

Maria is cleaning windows in the second floor master bedroom of the Armstrongs' house when she sees the gang in their green hoodies, legs propelling their skateboards up the curved driveway of the house next door. The white boy in the lead has a handsome, puckish face and a crowbar in his hand. A few strands of long red hair escape his hood, but his skin is almost as brown as her own.

He glances up before she can duck away and for a moment their gazes hold. She reads a promise in his eyes—the possibility of...*everything*—and an unfamiliar flutter moves in her chest.

He gives her a wink, then wedges the crowbar into the doorjamb by the lock. Wood splinters. The largest of the gang, a tall black man, kicks the door open like it's balsa wood. They all troop inside. Luz is last. Except for the white boy in the lead, none of the others have looked in her direction. A moment later the door shuts and it's like they were never there.

Maria half-expects an alarm to go off, but many homeowners in Desert View feel secure enough with the management of their gated community not to bother. Most criminals just pick easier targets.

She wonders how the hooded gang got past the guards. It doesn't matter how long she's been working here, she still has to show her I.D. every time the bus lets her off at the front gate, and the guard always checks her name against his list.

She looks up and down the street. No one seems to have noticed the intruders or even heard their boards as they rolled through the neighbourhood. In the barrio everyone notices everything, but here, people shut themselves away in their houses. Most are at work right now anyway.

She knows she should call 911. If it were happening to one of her clients, her cell would be out the moment she saw the gang turn into the driveway. But the people next door mean nothing to her. She doesn't even know their names.

She goes back to cleaning windows and thinks about how that white boy looked at her, how it felt like they were connecting on some deep level, if only for a moment. Then she thinks of Luz. She wonders what her relationship is to the gang. Specifically, to that handsome red-haired boy.

Luz.

Once upon a time they were best friends.

ONE NIGHT when they're fourteen, Luz comes tapping at the shutter of Maria's window. It's late, late. Past midnight, closer to dawn than not. Maria has been asleep for hours. Luz grins at her, bouncing on her toes like she's been chugging Redbulls all night.

Maria throws back the covers, then raises the window and leans out into the cool night.

"What are you *doing* out there?" she whispers.

"Stuff. Do you still have those silver and turquoise earrings we got at the thrift shop?"

Maria nods.

"Come on out," Luz says, "and bring them with you."

They bought the earrings together a few months ago at Buffalo Exchange, promising to share them like they do most of their fashion finds. When it's something special like these earrings, it's one week on and one week off. Maria knows a pang of disappointment. It's her turn this week and she's only had them for three days. She was going to wear them to school tomorrow.

But that's not the real problem.

"I can't come out," she says. "It's the middle of the night."

"Almost morning, actually."

Maria sighs. Luz can talk her into anything, so there's really not much point in fighting it.

"What are we going to do?" she asks.

"*Brujería.*"

Magic. The word hangs there in the air between them like the echo of a promise. Maria waits for the joke, but all Luz does is give her an impatient look.

"You're not going all boring on me, are you?" she asks.

There are many crimes in the law book Luz keeps in her head. Boring is on page one.

"Give me a sec'," Maria says and ducks back inside.

She leaves her tartan pajama bottoms on, but adds runners, a plain black T and a long-sleeved grey hoodie with a bulldog crest on the arm. She opens the cigar box where she keeps her jewellery and takes out the earrings. They're silver feathers with fine turquoise inlay that highlights the feather design. What a find they were. Vintage *Teme* Navajo, signed and everything. Not only are they beautiful, but they seem to weigh no more than a real bird's feather. Sighing, she puts them in her pocket and goes outside.

Luz leads her down to the dry wash where a couple of meth heads were found dead last week. This is forbidden territory. Not just by her parents, but by her older brother Pablo, too.

The chill desert air sends a shiver down Maria's spine. She looks around nervously, starting at every sound. An owl's hoot from the top of a distant saguaro. A packrat scurrying in the dry brush under the mesquite. Luz tramps down the sandy bottom of the wash with the comfortable stride of someone who simply assumes that she has every right to go wherever she wants.

When Maria catches up to her, Luz pulls out a small Player's cigarette tin with a cute sailor painted on it.

"What's that for?" Maria asks.

Luz opens it and points a small flashlight's beam inside. There's a picture in it from the photo booth at the mall, the two of them squished together, laughing.

"We're going to put the earrings in here," Luz says, "and then we're going to hide the tin. Years from now, when we've maybe gone our separate ways and one of us is looking for the other, she can retrieve the tin and it'll bring the other one back to her."

"But how?"

"*Brujería,*" Luz says like she did before, outside Maria's window.

She lifts the edge of the picture with a fingernail. At the bottom of the tin Maria sees a mix of things she can't identify. Powders and twigs, flower petals and bits of dried leaves.

"What is that stuff?" she asks.

"Pollen and barrio dust," Luz says. "Mixed with marigold petals, cactus thorns and mesquite leaves. Abuela gave me the spell. It only works if we don't tell anybody about it."

At that point Maria still thinks Luz means one of her grandmothers. She stares into the tin. The whole night feels haunted, like it's full of ghosts. Like she's walking on a thin mirror and any false step will make the glass shatter and she'll fall forever into some strange abyss. She shivers again and feels dizzy.

Maria blinks and the moment is gone. The world is as it should be once more, except that they're still in the forbidden dry wash with the dawn pinking the skies on the other side of the Hierro Madera Mountains.

"Are we really working magic?" she asks.

Luz nods. "Give me the earrings."

Maria takes them from her pocket and drops them into the cigarette tin that Luz holds out to her. Luz closes the tin with a snap and puts it in her pocket.

"Now we just have to hide it," she says, "and the spell is done."

"We can't hide it here," Maria says. "Somebody will find it."

"I know. We have to hide it in a place where, even if it's found, no one will dare to take it."

The only place Maria can think of like that is the head-quarters of the 66 Bandas—the local gangbangers. But when she mentions it, Luz shakes her head.

"I know a scarier place than that," she says. "The bottle man's yard."

Maria's eyes go wide.

The bottle man is a witch—a bottle witch who keeps his magic in the bottles he hangs in the trees around his home. He lives in a shack made of saguaro ribs and cast off pieces of tin and mismatched sizes of clapboard spray-painted with images of animals and pictographs in bright Oaxacan colours.

"Oh, I don't know," says Maria, a tremor in her voice. "They say he's loco and can make bad magic."

"Which is exactly why no one will ever find it there," says Luz, grabbing Maria by the hand and pulling her along the wash toward their destination.

Twenty minutes later they arrive at the bottle man's yard and stand quietly across the wash from his shack. It sits on the edge of the desert, an old mesquite tree towering above it, bottles of all shapes, sizes and colours tied to the branches where they tinkle softly when the wind taps them against each other.

The ground under the tree and all around the shack is thick with broken glass, but the pieces have no sharp edges. It's like they've been rolling against each other in an ocean for years until they're smoothed like pebbles, even though they actually come from when the monsoons blow hard and the bottles in the tree smash against each other.

Luz grins at Maria and pulls her into the yard. Maria's heart is pounding so loudly in her ears that she's certain that it, alone, will wake the sleeping bottle witch, but Luz proceeds steadily toward the river of broken glass. When they reach its edge, Luz lets go of Maria's hand and removes the tin and a clear sandwich bag from her pocket. She presses the tin against her lips, then offers it to Maria. Maria kisses it as well.

Luz seals the tin inside the bag, then removes one sandal and uses it to gently push aside the glass shards until a small well forms. Maria doesn't breathe, certain they are about to be caught by the bottle witch, but the sound of shifting glass only blends with the soft clink of bottles high in the tree branches above them. Luz places the tin in the hollow and smoothes the glass back over as quietly as she can. She slips her sandal back onto her foot, then reaches for Maria's hand and together they tiptoe back across the yard. When they reach the wash they run like cats being chased by coyotes.

MARIA HAS been cleaning the bedroom windows until she's afraid her hand will go right through the glass. But curiosity has the better of her. It's almost an hour later and the gang still hasn't come out of the house next door. If they're planning a "surprise party" for the owners, the busted door's a dead giveaway. If they're robbing the place, they're sure being choosy about what they take.

Finally she goes on to other work, glancing out windows on that side of the house whenever she can. By the time she's finished her day's work, the gang still hasn't emerged. As she locks the Andersons' door, Maria is tempted to peek in the windows next door to see what they're up to, but she doesn't risk it. She learned a long time ago that while minding your own business might be boring, it also keeps you alive.

She wonders if Luz still has that law book in her head: *The World According to Lucia Chaidez*. Back in the day, everything was Luz's business if it piqued her curiosity.

Maria walks down the street, takes one turn, then another. When she reaches the gate, the guard lets her out. She crosses the street and waits for the bus. A few moments later Connie sits down beside her, looking as tired as Maria feels. Connie undoes her hair, runs her fingers through it, then puts it back in a ponytail. She's dressed like Maria, in work clothes: sweats, T-shirt, sneakers. She leans back against the bench and stares up into the sky. Santo del Vado Viejo might be a city, but it's also in the desert. It's a desert sky up there, blue and sharp, and it goes on forever.

"The VVers are skating tonight," she says. "Are you going?"

Maria nods. She wants to say something about what she saw today, but the words feel locked on the tip of her tongue. Instead they talk about Baby Luna, the new jammer for Los Vampiros. They're still waiting for the bus when the first police car pulls up at the Desert View gates. They watch as two more vehicles enter the gated community.

"I wonder what's going on in there?" Connie says.

Maria shrugs. She's feeling a little bad about not having called 911—even if Luz was one of the gang invading the house next door. She doesn't care if the people who own it got robbed, but she doesn't want anybody to have been hurt.

"I'll bet it's Los Murrietas," Connie says. "They've been hitting gated communities all over the city."

Maria gives her a blank look.

"Everybody in the neighbourhood's talking about it. That's what this new gang is called."

"But what's it supposed to mean?"

"They're like Joaquin Murrieta. They only rob people like bank managers and CEOs. Poetic justice. None of those guys ever lose their own money—they just bleed the rest of us dry and collect their big bonuses. Supposedly, the gang has been giving most of the money they steal to people who've had mortgage foreclosures."

"For real?"

"I don't know. Nobody's ever come right out and said that's where they got the money. But I heard that's how Señora Morales was able to keep her house."

Maria wonders how Señora Morales explained her sudden windfall, but all she says is, "Cool."

HER ROOMMATE Veronica is still out when she gets home, but that's no surprise. Veronica works late more often than she doesn't—it's how you keep a job in this economy. Maria drops her knapsack on the floor and heads for the shower. When she comes out of the bathroom, drying her hair, she hears a knock at the door.

There's a cop standing in the hall—a black guy in a dark suit, white shirt, no tie, excellent hair. He shows her his badge. She doesn't look at it. She doesn't need to look at a badge to know he's a cop. Standing in the hall behind him is another one. This one's Hispanic. All she's wearing is an oversized T-shirt. He gives her an appreciative once-over but doesn't meet her gaze.

She leans against the doorframe, arms folded across her chest. She doesn't invite them in and they don't ask.

"Maria Martinez?" the black cop asks.

She nods.

"And you're an employee of Vado Viejo Maid Services?"

She nods again. She has an idea what this is about, but she's not going to make it easy for them.

"Your boss says you were working in the Anderson House in Desert View today."

"So?" she says.

She hopes nothing shows in her face.

"We were wondering if you saw anything unusual on the street while you were there."

She shakes her head. "Why? What happened?"

"The house next to where you were working was broken into this afternoon."

"If you saw anything, *chica*," the Hispanic cop adds, "now's the time to tell us. That way, maybe we won't put Immigration on your ass."

"Screw you," she tells him. "I was born here."

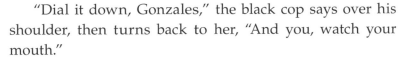

"Dial it down, Gonzales," the black cop says over his shoulder, then turns back to her, "And you, watch your mouth."

Maria gives him a cold look. "Are we done?"

"Almost. Are you sure you didn't see anything?"

"I was working. You don't exactly get time to daydream out a window if you're going to make your quota. Why are you pushing on this anyway? Since when does the law get all worked up about a simple break-in?"

"We take every crime seriously."

"And it's got nothing to do with it having happened in Desert View?"

"Of course not."

"So," she says, "let me get this straight. Last year my apartment got broken into and you guys did nothing. *Nada*. But a few weeks ago the cops shut down a party we were having and it wasn't even late. And now I'm supposed to give a crap about a bunch of rich gringos living in Desert View?"

The Hispanic cop frowns and takes a step forward, but his partner puts up a hand and he stops. The black cop sighs and hands her a business card.

"If you remember anything," he says, "call me."

Maria watches them until they turn into the stairwell. They're talking, but she only catches a bit of their conversation.

"…going to catch those bastards sooner or later."

She steps back inside her apartment. Closing the door, she tosses the business card in the trash.

WHEN THEY are fifteen, Luz gets suspended from school for fighting, which is completely unfair since she'd only been standing up to a bully. Maria says as much when she comes by Luz's house after school, but Luz only laughs.

"Don't you get it yet?" she says. "This is a life lesson."

Maria shakes her head. "No, I don't get it. Do you mean you shouldn't have stopped Blair from picking on Perlita?"

"Of course not," she says. She taps her index finger against Maria's forehead. "Think about it. This just reminds us that if you're rich and white, you can do whatever you want. You're always in the right. It's the brown-skinned girls like us who are always wrong."

"I hate this," Maria says.

Luz doesn't respond. She doesn't have to.

Maria points to some pebbles laid out in a line on the bedspread in between them.

"What are you doing with those?" she asks.

"It's something Abuela taught me."

By now Maria knows Luz doesn't mean either of her real grandmothers. She's talking about the old woman who lives in the small adobe building at the end of the block. Her yard is always full of stray dogs. She has the desert on one side of her, the headquarters of the 66 Bandas on the other, but the gang-bangers never bother her or her clients. They wouldn't dare.

That's because she's a *brujá*. She's like the bottle tree man, except her magic is in potions and the silver *milagros* she makes and sells. People use them to ask favours of the Saints. They're simple compared to the commercial kind in the stores, and they cost more, but everybody believes they work better so she has no lack of customers.

"They're magic stones?" Maria asks.

"Not yet. But she told me if you choose right, and if you carry that pebble around for a long time and fill it with the intent that it become magic, one day it will actually happen. And then you will be able to use that magic."

"*Verdad*?"

Luz nods.

"What are you going to do with it?" Maria asks.

"I don't know yet. Abuela says your intent has to be pure. I can't make my mind up yet, but I can focus on the pebble so that when it's ready, I'll be ready, too."

Maria's not sure what to think. Luz is always talking about *brujería* and the spirits. She says hawks are actually old men who have been drinking mescal tea to free their wings, and that some people walk around with animals under their skin. Maria believed the stories when she was younger. Now she's pretty sure that's all they are. Stories.

But still…

She points to a small black pebble that seems to hold the night just under its surface.

"That one," she says.

Luz smiles. "I thought so, too."

MARIA'S WITH her girls at the San Pedro Skating Center. She met Consuela through work. Veronica used to go out with Maria's brother and they stayed friends after the break-up, much to Pablo's annoyance. The girls sit on metal chairs, plastic cups of beer in hand, cheering for their team.

It's loud in the center. The wheels of the girls' skates on the wooden track compete with the shouting of the crowd and the band playing on the small stage on the far side of the center. The VVers are skating hard, but Los Vampiros' new jammer is in the zone and she's racking up the points. The girls should be unhappy that their team is losing, but like everyone else, they're entranced by the poetry of Baby Luna's movements as she darts and bobs in amongst the other girls on the track.

When the current jam is over the whole center erupts in spontaneous applause. It's the end of the second period. Baby Luna pumps a fist in the air, grinning at the crowd before she joins the rest of her team exiting the track.

"Man," Connie says. "Can that girl move."

Maria nods.

Veronica nudges her. "Hey. Check out the cute gringo checking *you* out."

Maria looks across the track and sees him immediately. It's the boy who was with Luz and the rest of the gang that robbed the house in Desert View. He's still wearing his green hoodie, but the hood's down, letting his red gold curls spill out to frame his face. He's even better looking than she remembers.

He grins and there's a knowing look in his eyes when he catches her gaze. She ducks her head. She has the oddest feeling that he can read her mind.

Veronica gives her another nudge.

"You should talk to him," she says. "Just go over and say hello."

"Yeah," Connie adds. "What've you got to lose?"

Everything, Maria thinks. She has no idea why that seems possible. But she gets up from her chair.

"Sure," she says. "Why not?"

Before she can lose her nerve, she's circling the track, aiming for where the handsome red-haired boy is sitting. His gaze tracks her movement, but she's feeling more confident now. It helps that she's turning a few heads along the way. She knows she looks good—much better than she did in the sweats she was wearing this afternoon while working: white tank with a fringed black vest, jean miniskirt, red cowboy boots. Her hair's up in a loose chignon, her makeup's light and fresh. A silver and turquoise Taxco bracelet that used to belong to her grandmother dangles on her wrist.

The red-haired boy has his crew sitting with him—there's a vibe that connects them all. It seems more like a brotherhood vibe than a gang thing, which is good because you don't bring a gang into 66 Bandas territory. To his right are two dark-haired barrio boys in skater shorts and oversized tees. To his left is the big black guy who kicked down the door of the place they robbed this afternoon. Dreadlocks frame his round face. On the next seat over is another red-haired white boy who could be the leader's brother or cousin. There's a family resemblance, but he's... prettier is the best way she can describe it. He doesn't have the same look of steel in his eyes that the leader does. The leader is the only one still wearing his green hoodie.

When she gets close enough, the black guy and the other red-haired boy move over a seat, leaving an empty chair beside the leader. The leader stands up, still smiling, but now he reaches out a hand. She takes it without thinking. He doesn't shake, he just holds her hand in his. His hand is warm and she doesn't want to take hers away. She feels like she might get lost in his hazel eyes.

"Great to see you again," he says, pulling her gently toward him.

She gets a little ping of worry. Are they going to spirit her away, use her up and then dump her in some arroyo so that she can't finger them to the cops? She wouldn't be the first.

But for some reason she trusts him.

"My name's Jack," he adds.

Then he introduces his crew. The barrio boys he calls the Glimmer Twins. She sees they're holding hands. She smiles at them. The black guy is Ti Jean and she can hear the Caribbean in his accent when he says hello.

"And that's my cousin Will," Jack adds, nodding to the other red-haired boy, who smiles back at her.

Maria can't quite place Jack's accent. It's British or Scottish, or some mix of the two. She imagines Will must sound like him.

"I'm Maria," she tells them.

She lets Jack steer her to the empty chair. She tugs at the hem of her skirt, but it's too short to make any difference. She presses her thighs close together.

"So how do you know Luz?" she says to Jack.

"Now that's a story," he says, "though it's not the easiest to tell. Lucia is a part of a lot of stories and they all kind of tangle into each other. Maybe we could go for a drink after the next bout and compare notes."

"What makes you think I'll go anywhere with five boys I don't know?"

"You could bring your friends," Ti Jean says.

Will nods. "Yes, you really ought to invite your friends," he says, his accent sounding like Jack's. "Why not call them over right now, so that we can meet them?"

"Maybe I will and maybe I won't," she says.

She's about to ask them where they're all from when she spots the person she's been looking for ever since Veronica pointed Jack out to her. Luz. She's standing at the front of the stage, just under a speaker. The band is rocking and Luz is grinning. She pumps a fist in the air to the infectious beat.

Maria leans closer to Jack and puts a hand on his shoulder.

"I need to see someone for a moment," she says. "Don't go away."

"Boy or girl?" Jack asks.

She looks at the Glimmer Twins, still holding hands.

"Does it matter?" she asks.

"Only to what could be," he tells her, looking right into her eyes.

She smiles.

"Hold that thought," she says.

She stands up and makes her way over to the stage.

WHEN THEY are sixteen, Luz shows up at Maria's house while Maria is making dinner. She slouches in a chair at the kitchen table and watches Maria cook tortillas in an iron frying pan. When each one is done, Maria puts it in a small quilted-cotton pouch that she keeps in the oven. On the stovetop is a pot of carne seca. Another holds a spicy mixture of beans and rice. Chopped tomatoes and lettuce and a heap of grated cheese wait on a cutting board.

"I'm going away," Luz says.

Maria has known for a long time that this day was coming. The barrio has always been too small to contain the force of nature that is Luz. She just didn't think it would be so soon.

"When?" she asks.

"Tonight."

"Where will you go?"

Luz shrugs. "I don't know. L.A. for starters."

"But what will you do there?"

"What are the two things I care about the most?"

"You mean beside looking good and having fun?"

Luz grins. "Styling and having fun—those are just a given. There's no point in living without them."

She takes out the black pebble that she's carried with her for over a year and shows it to Maria, holding it between her thumb and forefinger.

"I'm talking about magic," she says. "And fighting injustice."

"You can't fight injustice with magic," Maria says.

"Maybe you're right," Luz tells her. "But maybe not. I think it's all we've got left."

"And you're going to find magic in L.A.?"

"Probably not. But I've got to start somewhere. And Adelita has a place in Venice Beach, so I can crash with her for a week or so."

Maria wants to beg her not to throw her life away for something that doesn't exist. Magic's only in stories and there is no justice for brown-skinned girls like them. But she knows Luz too well. She can't be talked out of something like this.

"Good luck," she says.

Maria doesn't see her again until Luz is robbing the banker's house in Desert View.

MARIA'S NOT sure what sort of a welcome she can expect from Luz. It's been a few years now and clearly their lives have gone in very different directions. She's a maid working in rich people's homes. Luz robs those same houses. They probably have nothing in common anymore.

But Luz's eyes light up as soon as she catches sight of Maria. She enfolds her in a tight embrace.

She says something, but Maria can't hear her over the band. Maria motions towards the door and mouths, "Let's go outside!"

Luz nods and they leave the center. The desert night is cool and the breeze coming in from the Hierro Madera Mountains feels good on their skin. It's quieter, too, though they can still hear the band. There are people all around, smoking and talking.

"You look amazing," Luz says.

"So do you."

And she does. She's sleek and trim, her hair twisted into a long braid that hangs halfway down her back. Her capris ride low on shapely hips and a sleeveless T shows off muscular arms.

"How long have you been back?" Maria adds.

"Not long. I wanted to come see you, but…"

Luz's voice trails off.

"You didn't want me to get involved with your gang," Maria finishes for her.

"You know about that?"

Maria nods. "I saw you guys break into that house today."

A big smile spreads across Luz's face.

"*You're* the hot tamale that Jack's been going on about?" she says.

For a moment Maria allows herself to be distracted. "He called me a hot tamale?"

"He hasn't stopped talking about you. He says you're his missing half." She bumps a fist against Maria's shoulder. "And that's after only one glance."

Maria tilts her head toward the center. "I was just talking to him inside," she says.

Luz studies her for a moment and the big smile comes back. "*Ai yi yi.* You like him, too!"

Maria feels a hot flush rising up her neck.

"What are you doing?" she says to change the subject. "How can you have joined a gang? We always hated the bandas."

"I didn't join a gang," Luz says. "I *started* one. And we're doing this to even the playing field between the haves and have-nots."

"By stealing?"

Luz sighs. "Remember the pebble and what Abuela told me about it?"

Maria nods.

"I used it to bring a spirit to me."

"A spirit."

Maria tries to keep the disbelief from her voice. Luz doesn't seem to notice.

"I was trying for someone like Joaquin Murrieta," Luz says, "or even El Zorro. You know, take from the rich and give to the poor?"

"You're really doing that?"

"Of course. I'm not a thief—at least I'm not robbing anyone for my own benefit. I knew I couldn't rally the people to my cause—I mean, who's Lucia Chaidez? I needed a figurehead that they could recognize. But when I called for the kind of spirit I wanted, who I got was Robin Hood."

"Robin Hood."

Luz nods. "Except he calls himself Jack Green."

Maria glances back to the center. "You mean Jack, in there..?"

She wants to think her friend has gone a little loco since she went away. Because how can such a thing be possible? But this is Luz, and Luz could always make the improbable happen.

"And it's not just Jack," Luz says. "He brought his crew with him."

"He wants to go for a drink later," Maria finds herself saying. "I'm here with Connie and Veronica."

"The same Veronica who goes out with Pablo?"

Maria nods. "Except they broke up and now she's my roommate. And Connie's a friend from work."

"What do they know?" Luz asks.

"About what you...do? Nothing."

"Then we should all go for that drink."

"You know the police are looking for you, right?"

"They're looking for Los Murrietas," Luz says. "Not us. They don't know who we are."

"The cops came by to question me because I was working next door. They wanted to know if I'd seen anything."

"What did you tell them?"

"What do we ever tell them?"

"Good for you."

"But you need to be careful," Maria says. "They seem pretty determined to catch you guys."

"That's why we wear the hoods. They can't identify us. And even if they got a face, they couldn't match it to anything. The boys are all spirits."

Maria's still not exactly sure what that means. Everything about Jack seemed very real to her. His eyes, his warmth.

"But *you're* real," she says.

"This is true. I'll just have to be careful. And you should be, too. Jack can be a lot of fun, but you have to remember he's just an archetype. It's not like he's a real boy."

"What's that supposed to mean?"

"Nothing. Never mind. We'll just have some fun. Let's go back inside. I think the next bout is starting up."

EVERYBODY HITS it off. Connie and Veronica are as delighted with Ti Jean and Will as the boys are with them. Jack is full of good humour and more attentive to Maria than any guy she's been with before. The Glimmer Twins are content with each other. And if Luz feels like the odd woman out, she doesn't show it.

Los Vampiros clean up in the last period, but there was never any doubt that the The VVers were going to lose tonight. They played their hardest ever, but they didn't stand a chance with Baby Luna so in the zone.

Maria, Luz, Maria's girls and their new friends whoop and cheer, then go to the taquería around the corner to continue the party. Maria and the girls have to work tomorrow, but they're having too much fun to call it a night. This won't be the first time they go in tired and a little hungover.

The boys can drink, but it doesn't seem to affect them. They seem particularly fond of hard liquor—tequila, Scotch and Irish whiskey being the favourites. At one point Jack holds a shot of tequila up to the light and peers through the clear liquid before downing it.

"Veritably," he says, "this is the nectar of the gods."

Maria and her girls exchange glances, then laugh. Who talks like that?

He motions to the bartender for another. Maria doesn't even try to keep up with him.

THEY ALL end up back at Maria and Veronica's apartment. Because of the visit the cops paid her earlier in the day, Maria worries that they might be watching their building, but she doesn't see anything suspicious.

Veronica's laptop is hooked up to a sound system in the living room. She picks a playlist, turns the volume down low, and a moment later one of Malo Malo's quieter songs comes out of the speakers. She's been watching Jack all night, trying to figure out what Luz means about him not being real. Maria decides to stop worrying. She takes Jack by the hand and leads him through the kitchen and out the back door to the fire escape.

He lifts her hand to his lips and kisses the back of it, then turns it over and kisses her palm. Oh yes, he's real enough. The gentle warmth of his lips stirs her more than any groping embrace could. She puts her hand behind his head and their lips finally meet in a soft kiss. Then his hand is up the back of her shirt, making tingly circles on the bare skin of her back. She reluctantly pulls away when it begins to edge around to her front.

"Not when we haven't even had a proper date," she says, smiling at him.

They both know that sooner or later they'll end up in bed together, but Maria doesn't want to come across as some loose *chica* who would put out on a first date—especially since they haven't even *had* a date yet. And this isn't the right time or setting. She knows she's too tipsy. Jack is definitely drunk—or he should be, considering how much he consumed this evening. Her apartment is full of people, many of them wanted by the police.

But Jack is so damned handsome.

They gaze at each other—Maria can literally feel the air spark between them—then Jack smiles.

"Fair enough," he says. "I can wait."

She leans back into his shoulder. It feels good. It feels like they fit together, as though this is meant to be.

"This is such a strange world," he says.

She pulls back and looks up at him, not quite sure what he means or how to respond.

"There's so much noise," he goes on. "It never stops. Cars and voices and TVs. I can even hear the electricity in the wires. The humming is constant."

"You should go out into the desert," she says. "Get out far enough and all you can hear is the wildlife and the wind."

"I've been. Lucia took us when we first got here. And that was strange in another way. She said she was bringing us to a forest, but there was no green wood like at home. It was all giant cacti."

"It's a saguaro forest," she tells him. She waits a beat, then adds, "Where's your home?"

"Farther away than you could ever imagine."

He hasn't answered her question and Maria doesn't press him. There's a wistful note in his voice. She finds herself thinking again about magic pebbles and spirits, and Luz saying Jack wasn't a real boy.

She leans into his shoulder once more and closes her eyes. If this isn't real, she doesn't know what is.

WHEN SHE opens her eyes again she's lying on top of her bedspread, still fully dressed. It's morning. The apartment is quiet.

Last night feels like a dream.

She looks at the clock beside her bed.

"Oh crap," she says.

She's going to be late for work. She taps on the door to Veronica's room on her way to take a shower. It isn't until she's back in her own room getting dressed that she notices the note on the night table.

See you tonight for a real date? 8 pm at the taquería?

She's still smiling when she runs out to catch her bus.

VERONICA LAUGHS when she comes home that night to find Maria preening in front of the mirror.

"Look at you," she says. "Somebody's got a hot date. Anybody I know?"

"Jack."

"At least he called you. Ti Jean said he would, but he never did."

"I'm sorry."

Veronica shrugs, then cocks her head to one side. "You wearing that?"

Maria's heart sinks. She looks in the mirror at the short, tight green dress she's trying on. The heels that hurt her feet. She chose the green for Jack, like she's wearing his gang colours.

"Too much?" she asks, knowing the answer.

"Depends. It's okay if you're going somewhere fancy, but if you're just hanging out, it's not really *you*. You look pretty, but a little too chi-chi. He might as well know right off the bat that you're edgier than that."

Maria nods and gives Veronica a quick hug. She kicks off the heels, adds black leggings and floral patterned Doc Marten boots.

"Now *there's* my girl," Veronica says, beaming with satisfaction. "Those Docs were worth saving up for. You look great."

THIS TIME of year the night comes early. The rains usually arrive in October or November, but the skies have been clear for days. The days have been warm, the nights cool.

By the time Maria arrives at the taquería, the shadows are lengthening. The sun has almost dropped below the horizon. Jack is waiting for her outside the restaurant. He leans with his back against a patio railing, his skateboard on the ground by his feet. He gives her an appreciative smile as she approaches, but her own smile dies when the pleasure in his eyes turns to steel.

"The cops have Lucia," he says.

Maria feels as though she's been punched in the chest.

"What…how did they find her?" Maria asks.

"We were casing a way into Silver Canyon."

Silver Canyon. Another gated community. Open to anyone who can afford the starting prices of three million.

"Did they get any of the others?" Maria asks.

He shakes his head. "Just Lucia. She was doing a walk-by while we were waiting in the brush across from the gatehouse. The guard must have gotten suspicious and called the cops." He puts a hand on her arm. "I'm sorry, Maria. We should have been more careful."

"They can't hold her for nothing! When is she being arraigned? Does she have a lawyer?"

"You know they'll hold her as long as they can."

Maria shakes her head. "They can't do that. She has rights."

"No, she doesn't. None of us do. We're not rich enough."

Maria just stares at him.

"Come on," he says. "How do you think the D.A. and sheriff got elected? It's the rich who fund their war chests, and if the people we robbed want someone in jail, that's what the sheriff's going to give them."

Maria thinks of something Luz once said to her.

If you're rich and white, you can do whatever you want. You're always in the right. It's the brown-skinned girls like us who are always wrong.

"Then what can we do?" she says.

"Ti Jean wants to break her out of county."

"Can we do that?"

Jack raises an eyebrow at her use of 'we,' but all he says is, "Sure. If we had an army and guns and enough explosives to blow our way in."

"Don't make fun of me."

"I'm not. I want her out as much as you do."

Maria studies him for a moment.

"But you've got magic," she says.

He shakes his head. "No, I don't."

"Luz told me you were spirits—that she called you up—and spirits have magic."

"Maybe they do. But we're not spirits. We're…" He sighs. "I'm not sure what we are. I only know we used to live in a green wood and something brought us here. To this life."

"You mean Luz."

"I don't know who or what brought us here," Jack says. "Half of me remembers growing up in the north of England with Will, and then moving to South London where we hooked up with Ti Jean. We met the Glimmer Twins in Venice Beach. Then we found Lucia, or she found us.

"But at the same time, we all remember another life in the green wood. Or maybe it's merely a dream we all share because a lot of it doesn't make sense. The trees were more than shelter. I think we slept inside them and our…vitality rose and fell with the passing of the seasons."

Maria doesn't like the lost look in his eyes.

"Luz said you're an archetype," she finds herself saying.

"Huh." He considers that for a moment before he asks, "What do you think?"

"I don't know what to think. I'm not even sure I know what that means."

"Well, I can tell you this much. If there's any magic around, it belongs to Lucia." He waits a beat, then adds, "And maybe to you."

"To *me*?"

Jack nods. "That's what Lucia says."

"How would she know something like that? Luz hasn't seen me in years."

"Yet here you are, willing to drop everything to help her."

"She's still my friend," Maria says. "She was my best friend."

"I admire loyalty in a person. In the end, our integrity is the only thing of value that no one can take from us. It's the reason we support Lucia's cause."

"Which seems really complicated."

"Actually, it's not," Jack says. "It's simple, really. A banker uses deceit to rob you and he gets rewarded with a bailout from the government and a bonus from his shareholders. You or me? We go to jail. Since the law isn't on our side, we have to take matters into our own hands. It's up to us to balance the wealth."

"It's not that simple."

"Of course it isn't," Jack says. "But we have to start somewhere. Lucia says that the first thing we have to do is get their attention. So we've left messages behind in all the places we hit. We also sent letters of explanation to the papers and television and radio stations."

"The Occupy Wall Street people aren't robbing houses to get attention."

"No," Jack says. "But they're treated as a joke, just as we are when they call us Los Murrietas. Nobody takes our messages seriously. They make us sound like just another gang, robbing honest, hard-working citizens instead of the bankers and CEOs."

"Why wouldn't the media report that? Wouldn't it make a good story?"

"I don't know, but the banks hold a lot of sway and even reporters don't want to get on the bad side of them. Everyone needs their banker to be on their side. So the truth is being suppressed.

"Somehow, we have to make the public really sit up and take notice of why we're doing what we do."

Maria's torn. She's spent her whole life trying not to be noticed. And what has it gotten her? A job as a maid. Maria doesn't necessarily agree with the gang's methods, but at least they're doing something that has real meaning.

"We have to get Luz out," she says.

Jack nods. "But we can't do it legally."

"And we don't have an army."

Maria doesn't say anything more.

Jack prompts her. "Which leaves only..."

The impossible, Maria wants to say. But then she thinks of a black pebble on a bedspread.

And she thinks of a tin cigarette box.

"*Brujería*," she says.

"Broo-what?"

"Magic."

MARIA LEADS the way through the barrio streets to where the last buildings meet the desert, Jack at her side. The rest of his gang has joined them, and are trailing slightly behind. Without going into detail, Maria explains that she and Luz have a pact to fulfill and she needs to retrieve a talisman to do it. She'd like to share the whole story, but Luz said that it would only work if they told no one.

Any other part of town and the desert scrub beyond these adobe buildings would have become a swath of gated communities and shopping plazas. But here, right on the edge of 66 Bandas territory, nobody's stupid enough to try to build. Past the city limits, a few ranches and adobe houses make a patchwork buffer zone between the barrio and the national park in the foothills of the Hierro Madera Mountains.

Maria is not happy. The only good thing about tonight is having Jack beside her holding her hand. She wishes they could just keep walking and leave everything behind. That her companions weren't robbers. That Luz wasn't in jail. That it wasn't her responsibility to try to make things right.

But the past is like the desert lying hidden under the green lawns and streets of the gated communities like Silver Canyon and Desert View. You can disguise it with a cover of manicured grass and pavement, but the desert doesn't go away. It's still there underneath, waiting to be free again.

When they reach a dry wash, she turns south along its sandy bed and they all follow suit. That her companions took her story at face value doesn't surprise her. After all, how odd can magic be to spirits?

But while they can just accept the notion of seeking a talisman, what fills them with wonder is the appearance of the bottle man's tree: all its glass vessels dangling from the widespread branches of the old mesquite, each glowing in the moonlight so that it seems to hold rather than reflect the light. Across the yard, a small sea of glass pebbles shimmers between the wash where they stand and the bottle man's shack.

Even after all these years Maria is pretty sure she remembers the general area where the tin would be—if it's still there—but she needs to gather up her nerve to actually enter the yard to look for it. She takes a breath, but before she can take that first step, Jack puts a hand on her arm.

"Wait," he says. "I've seen places like this before. Well, not exactly like *this*. The ones in the green wood were mostly stoneworks, half covered by forest growth. But this *feels* the same."

"How so?"

"Prickly. Full of magic. Protective magic. We should ask permission before we enter."

Maria bites her lip. She doesn't like this place any more than she did the last time she came.

They hear a soft scuff in the dirt behind them.

"I was wondering when one of you would show up," a gravely voice says.

Maria turns to find a stranger

standing on the bank of the wash. He's an old man wearing raggedy cotton trousers and a flimsy grey T-shirt that is so tattered and faded, its logo is no longer recognizable. His hair is grey, too, and hangs in long thin ropes on either side of his dark brown face. It flows down his back like strands of mistletoe falling from the branches of a palo verde tree. He has more wrinkles than sun-baked mud, and his eyes are so dark they seem black. His mouth is a straight line, neither smiling nor frowning.

This can only be the bottle witch.

Maria starts to say something, but her throat has gone completely dry. Jack gives her fingers a light squeeze.

"Wh-what do you mean?" she finally croaks.

"Did you really think I wouldn't know when something new is added to my collection?" the bottle man says. "The only reason I let it remain is that I like the taste of your magic." He runs his tongue over his lips and leers at Maria.

"Can I please get it back?" she asks. "I need it to help my friend."

"What if I say no? Did you bring these *caballeros* to make sure you get your way? To keep you safe from me?"

"Oh no," Maria says.

"Why?" the bottle man says, edging closer so that she can smell his foul body odor. "Don't you think I'm dangerous?"

Maria feels like she's stepped into quicksand. That no matter what she says, she will sink.

"Everybody knows not to bother you," she tells him. "My friend and I meant you no harm when we buried the tin box here, and I mean you no harm now. I only came to get it back."

"And why should I trust you—an intruder who travels with a pack of foreign foxes?"

Maria can only stare at the bottle man in confusion.

"I'm not sure what you mean," she says.

"He means he can smell the green wood in us," Jack says.

"And," Ti Jean adds, stepping up beside them, "he's working up to telling you what he wants in trade for having stored that box of yours for all these years."

The bottle man nods toward Ti Jean and a slow smile creeps across his face. His whole body seems to vibrate with anticipation.

"But I don't have anything to trade," Maria says.

"That's not true," Jack says, "but what you have, I won't allow him to take. Neither your body nor your soul."

The bottle man spits on the ground and scowls at Jack. "She's not yours to bargain with, fox."

He turns back to Maria, the smile returning. "Come inside. I merely want one night with you and then you can take the box."

Maria cringes in horror. "Never," she says.

Jack put his arm around her shoulders and juts his chin toward the bottle man. "You heard her. So why don't we wager, you and I? Some contest of skill to decide how this will go."

The bottle man shakes his head. "I know a marksman when I see him. I don't have such skills."

"Then appoint a proxy."

The bottle man shakes his head again. "I have a better wager. Tell me my name in three guesses or less and you can have that box. If not, it stays with me."

He looks at Maria and licks his lips again. "Unless you'd like to change your mind, *chica*."

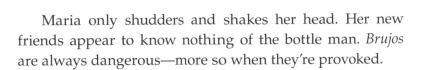

Maria only shudders and shakes her head. Her new friends appear to know nothing of the bottle man. *Brujos* are always dangerous—more so when they're provoked.

The witch extends a bony finger toward them. "Then leave. I'll keep the box. You have nothing to offer me."

"But we haven't even agreed to a wager yet," Jack says. "Something you could certainly gain from, should you be the victor. What have you to lose?"

The bottle man's face swivels back and forth as he tries to read Jack. It's clear that his interest is piqued. "I don't have all night," he says.

Jack smiles. "Finally, some common ground because neither do we. But let me propose another option that requires neither skill nor wit. Let us *pay* for the box."

"I have no need for money."

"Did I say money? I thought instead that we could earn your goodwill. Have you some chore that needs doing? At a later date, of course, since we've already agreed that time is pressing for both of us tonight."

The bottle man shakes his head. "A trick if I ever heard one. And who's to say you would keep your end of the bargain?"

Jack stands straighter and places his palm against his own chest.

"Now you wound me," he says. "I may have neither home nor riches, but I have my honour. As a man of my word, I resent any implication to the contrary. You insult my integrity."

"But—"

Jack holds up a hand. "One moment. We cannot continue our earlier business until we address this besmirchment of my good name. I name Ti Jean as my second. You, sir, as the challenged party may choose the weapons and, of course, your own second."

"Wait a minute…"

"Unless," Jack goes on, "you wish to tender something else in exchange for the apology that you now owe me."

"*Owe* you?"

Jack smiles. "Surely you see my predicament? You are indebted to me for my honour."

The bottle man returns his smile. "What I see is that you think if you talk fancy enough and long enough that I'll give you what you want because I'll be too exasperated to do anything else. It's not going to work."

"Fair enough," Jack tells him. "Since we can't come to a reasonable agreement between the two of us, we'll have to seek council elsewhere. Isn't there a wise woman living here in the barrio?"

The bottle man frowns. "Maybe you didn't notice that I'm not inclined to socialize."

Jack goes on as if the bottle man hasn't spoken. "A Señora Esmeralda? I believe the people call her Abuela." He smiles. "Just as they call you Abuelo. But we both know that women are always more powerful than men—especially when it comes to *brujería*."

Maria looks at Jack and wonders where he learned these things.

The bottle man spits again on the dirt. "Don't try my patience," he says, eyes narrowed.

"I don't mean to," Jack assures him. "The sooner we get this settled with an impartial third party, the sooner we can get back to our earlier negotiation. And time *is* pressing."

The bottle man grunts. "Señora Esmeralda has no business in this."

"So you'd prefer to duel?"

"I'd prefer you to take that damn box and never return to bother me again."

Jack arches his eyebrows. "No strings attached?"

"No strings."

"You are indeed a gentleman," Jack says.

"And you are plainly a cousin of Coyote."

"I will take that as a compliment," Jack tells him.

The bottle man shakes his head and turns away. He walks across the sea of glass pebbles as steadily as he might on solid ground. A few feet from his shack he reaches down into the glass with his fingers. He retrieves the cigarette tin and removes it from its plastic bag, which he stuffs in his pocket. The scowl on his face could sour milk, but he makes his way slowly back across the yard toward the wash.

"Thank you, señor," Jack says, reaching for the box.

But the bottle man shoves it toward Maria instead, grabbing hold of her fingers in the process. His black eyes are narrowed and his rough hand squeezes hers until it hurts.

"Now go away," he says, releasing her fingers. "And take these annoying foxes with you."

Maria nods. "*Gracias*," she murmurs, "*gracias*." But he's already turned and shuffling back toward his shack.

Maria's hand is still aching from being squeezed, but she gets a nail in under the edge of the lid. As it pops it open, she starts to fall. Ti Jean is closest and catches her, gently lowering her to the ground. Will catches the tin as it tumbles from her hand. Jack starts for her, but then turns and yells at the bottle tree man.

"You said no strings! What did you do to her?"

The bottle man turns back. "I did nothing. Those girls did it to themselves. But why are you surprised? When it comes to magic, we both know that women are always more powerful than men."

Chuckling at his own joke, he turns away again.

Jack wants to go after him, but he takes a steadying breath and kneels down beside Maria.

He puts his lips to her ear. "Where have you gone?" he whispers.

"What do we do now?" one of the Glimmer Twins asks.

The others all look at Jack.

Jack sits cross-legged beside Maria. He folds his hoodie and puts it under her head.

"Let's see that tin," he says to Will.

He puts it in her hands, then cups them with his own.

"Maybe closing it will undo the spell," he says.

But when the tin snaps shut there's no change. Jack sighs and puts the tin in his pocket. He takes Maria's hands again and looks at his men.

"I guess we wait," he says.

MARIA REMEMBERS opening the cigarette box in the wash near the barrio, the night sky tall with stars above her, Jack and the rest of his gang leaning in close to see what's inside. Now she's on her own, standing on an unfamiliar beach. It's still night, but everything looks and smells wrong. Or at least different. A boardwalk runs along the edge of the beach and she spies a lone figure sitting on a bench, looking out over the ocean. The sound of the tide is like the universe breathing, slow and steady.

Maria walks toward the bench.

"Luz?" she says as she draws near.

Luz turns. Her face lights up with happy recognition.

"Oh, hey, Maria," she says. "What are you doing here?"

The question catches Maria off-guard.

"I'm not sure," she says. "I don't even know where here is."

Luz's only response is to pat the wooden slats of the bench beside where she is sitting.

"Do you ever get that sense that everything happens for a reason?" she says.

Maria slowly closes the distance between them and lowers herself onto the bench beside her friend. She's not interested in a philosophical discussion right now.

"Where are we?" she asks. "The last thing I remember is opening that little tin cigarette box we left in the bottle tree man's yard back when we were kids."

"So *that's* why you're in my dream," Luz says.

Maria shakes her head. "I'm pretty sure I'm me—not some version of me that you're dreaming."

"Of course you're you. I just meant you've come to visit me in my dream. I'm still asleep back in my cell at county."

"I'm not asleep," Maria says. "I'm…"

She was about to say that she's in the wash by the bottle tree man's yard, but the truth is, she doesn't know where she is or how she got here. The last thing she remembers is opening that cigarette tin.

"This is more of your magic," she says.

Luz shakes her head. "*Our* magic. We made this spell together."

Maria wants to say that she doesn't know anything about magic, except she's here, isn't she? She opened the cigarette tin and—just like that—she was transported from the wash to…to wherever she is now. So instead of arguing, she decides to focus on the reason she wanted to see Luz. Everything else can wait until things are back to normal. If they ever get back to normal.

"The—" She stumbles over the next word, but goes on. "—*spell* was supposed to bring you to me. Not the other way around. It was supposed to rescue you."

"I'm pretty sure it wasn't," Luz says. "It was just supposed to bring us together and that's what it did. And maybe you should appreciate being in my dream instead of my cell in county. That place is pretty sketchy."

"I wouldn't know."

Luz laughs. "Of course you wouldn't. But I don't need to be rescued. I'm small potatoes. I have no record and they probably can't prove anything. Just get the guys to do a bigger score and set some aside for my bail. Then you come and bail me out. I know how to disappear after that."

Maria doesn't like where this is going. "Another robbery. You want to make this worse?"

Luz nods. "Oh, you don't have to be involved beyond posting bail. Just tell Jack and his merry band of men that they have to do at least one more score, and make it big."

"I can't believe this. How can you even think about doing more?" Maria asks.

"Well," Luz says, "there's a widow with MS on 42nd Street who's about to lose her home if we don't get some back payments to her.

"And then there's a long distance driver who's going to lose his rig because his wife got sick and he borrowed against it to pay for her hospital care. Did you know that the cab alone for those things can cost up to a-hundred-and-forty K?"

"But—"

Luz doesn't let her interrupt. "The trouble is," she goes on, "long-distance hauling is down—like everything else in this economy—and there's no way he can catch up unless we help him."

"How did this become *your* responsibility?" Maria asks.

"It should be everybody's," Luz tells her, "but too many people just think about themselves these days. So I'm redistributing the wealth."

"You should have been robbing the banks instead of bankers."

Luz nods. "Sure, except the point is to take their *own* money and redistribute *it*. Make it personal. Hit them where it hurts. Maybe then they'll understand that there are actual people just like them being affected by what they do. Nothing else seems to work."

"I don't know..."

"So nobody you know's been hurt by the banks and the big corporations and a government that doesn't give a crap?"

Maria thinks of all the unemployed people in her neighbourhood. All the people who've lost homes along with their jobs. And that's on top of third- and fourth-generation Hispanic citizens being treated like illegals by the cops, having to show papers every time they turn around, while no one else gets asked.

Luz and Jack are right. Somehow they've got to send a message that real people are being hurt. This all reminds her of something else—how she never used to give money to homeless people, but Veronica always has. When she finally asked her roommate why, Veronica said, "Because there, but for the grace of Our Lady, go you or I."

After that, Maria started giving, too. And she began talking to those people and seeing them as individuals, rather than as some nameless bunch of panhandlers. So many told her they never imagined that they'd be driven to ask for charity. And lately, things have only been getting worse.

"I'm in," says Maria. "What can I do to help?"

"Just give Jack my message," Luz says. "That's all."

"I can do that."

"Thanks," Luz says. "The sooner they get started, the sooner I can be out of here." She lifts a finger and moves it toward Maria's brow, adding, "So you'd better get to it."

When the pad of Luz's finger touches Maria's skin, everything goes away. Now she's back in the wash, lying in the dirt with Jack looking down at her with a worried expression.

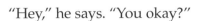

"Hey," he says. "You okay?"

Maria feels disoriented.

"I don't know," she says.

He eases her slowly into a sitting position. For a moment she thinks she can hear the ocean, but the sensation fades. She looks from Jack to the others, trying to find some sense in what she'd just experienced.

"What happened?" she asks.

"You fainted," Will tells her.

"It didn't feel like that," Maria says. "It felt like I went away. I was here and then I was with Luz. She said I'd gone into a dream she was having."

Her companions exchange glances.

"I know, I know," she says. "It sounds *loco*. But it felt real."

"It was magic," one of the Glimmer Twins whispers.

"It was something like that," Maria agrees.

She goes on to tell them what happened when she met Luz. What she thinks happened. She's not sure anymore. But her companions take it in stride.

"It makes sense," Ti Jean says.

The rest of them nod.

"But the hit has to be somewhere we haven't been before," Will says. "They'll be watching Desert View and Silver Canyon."

"There's that place in Sycamore Creek," one of the Glimmer Twins says. "The one we were checking out last week."

"I've got a better idea," Jack says. "Let's hit the sheriff's house."

No one says anything for a long moment, then they all break into laughter and start slapping Jack on the back.

"When do we go?" Maria asks.

Jack shakes his head and squeezes her shoulder. "This is what *we* do. Right now you should just walk away while you can."

"Is that really what you want me to do? Walk away...like we never met?"

"It's dangerous," Jack says.

Maria smiles. "Maybe I am, too."

Jack looks into her eyes, studying her hard. Then he puts a hand behind her head and gives her a fierce kiss. When he pulls away, Maria's head is swimming.

Jack jumps to his feet and gives her a hand up.

"Let's go!" he cries.

He leads the way back down the wash at a brisk jog. The rest of them follow, Maria right at his side.

IT'S NOT hard to find where the sheriff lives. Ted Crase isn't shy about publicity—doesn't matter if it's good or bad, so long as they spell his name right. There have always been whispers of corruption surrounding his election and rumours of payoffs from the bandas, but nothing that has ever been proven.

His house is deep in El Rio Valley, a gated community in the north part of the city. Its twelve-foot concrete wall, complete with ostentatious castle ramparts, looks ridiculous here in the desert. It also gives the appearance of being impenetrable, but getting over it is easier than Maria expected. One of the Glimmer Twins puts his foot in the stirrup Ti Jean makes with his hands, then Ti Jean shoots him above his head in one swift motion. The small figure seems to fly to the top of the wall. He fusses up there for a moment as he loops a rope around a rampart and tosses it down.

One by one they go up, the boys scrambling like monkeys. Maria is slower, but she's done this before. The difference between now and climbing ropes in the gym back in school is that tonight it's fun. She drops the last few feet and lands lightly on the grass.

Anglos, she's noticed, can be divided into two types: the ones that embrace Southwestern culture and the desert, at times almost to the point of being obnoxious about it, and those that try to reshape the desert into the same landscape as wherever they came from. A lawn like this on a golf course? She may not agree with it, but she gets that. But here in your backyard?

This time there are no skateboards clattering on the pavement. Instead they move through the backyards like ghosts. Beyond the community's stone walls, the yards are fenced in, but everybody must get along since the gates between them are only closed with latches. But there's still security.

Jack leads the way. He seems to have a sixth sense about motion sensors and which places have a dog. It's late and quiet, and the houses are mostly dark. Everything stays that way until they're in Sheriff Crase's backyard.

Maria listens to the boys as they study the house.

"Surveillance cameras on either corner."

"I see them. Probably in front, too."

"Alarms on all the windows. The doors will be wired."

"Motion detectors on the ground floor."

"Nobody home." That's from Will. He cocks his head, then adds, "Except...maybe a cat?"

Jack nods. "Definitely a cat."

"How can you *know* all that?" Maria asks. "We're just sitting here in the backyard. You haven't even walked up to the house yet."

Jack smiles. "You have your magic, we have ours."

"It's what we do," one of the Glimmer Twins explains.

"And we've been doing it for a long long time," the other twin adds. He gives Maria a grin. "Now watch this."

The twins leap up onto the fence surrounding the yard and walk along its narrow edge toward the house as though they're simply ambling through one of the wide dusty roads in the barrio. They take turns springing lightly from the fence top onto the roof, then one of them holds the other's legs as he dangles off the edge, fiddling with some box.

"Show-offs," Ti Jean mutters, but he's smiling.

Maria can't see what the twins do with the box, but after a few moments an owl hoots. Maria is startled by how close the bird sounds, then realizes the owl call was made by one of the twins. At the signal, Jack and Will emerge from the shadows on either side of her and start across the lawn toward the patio and its waiting glass doors. Maria hurries along behind until she catches up.

"How does a sheriff even afford a place like this?" Will says as they step onto a back patio as big as Maria's whole apartment.

"Cattle money," she tells him. "His family used to have this huge ranch north of the city."

Jack is at the glass doors. He inserts a couple of thin strips of metal into the lock. He works them for a moment, then the lock clicks open. The Glimmer Twins swing down from the roof and land softly on the patio. A moment later and they're all inside. The room is cavernous—easily as large as the patio—with the shapes of furniture crouching around the centrepiece of a large stone fireplace.

"Is there a safe?" Jack asks.

Ti Jean lifts his head, nostrils working.

"Front of the house," he says. "On the left."

Maria doesn't even bother to question how they do it anymore.

Jack pulls a couple of spray paint cans from the pockets of his jacket and tosses them to the twins.

"Have fun," he says as he follows Ti Jean and Will to the front of the house.

Maria waits where she is. She watches the twins spray messages on the white adobe walls of the living room and feels sorry for the maid who's going to have to clean this up.

One of the twins writes: "Give back to the poor."

The other writes: "Los Murrietas help you to share!"

When they start to tag the other walls, Maria goes to the front of the house where the other boys are. She walks carefully in the dark, though the streetlights out front help illuminate the house, so her eyes adjust quickly.

Maria enters a room where the boys have pulled a painting from the wall, revealing a safe. Jack leans close to it, smiling as he turns the tumblers. There's a final click and Jack steps back with a flourish of his arm. Will laughs and pulls open the door of the safe. They all step closer to look inside.

"Holy crap," Ti Jean says.

He reaches in and takes out a bundle of money, flipping through a stack of one-thousand-dollar bills. Maria's never seen that much money in her entire life. She's never even seen that denomination before.

"There's got to be a half a mil," Will says, then he turns at Maria. "Cattle money?" he teases.

Maria shakes her head. There's only one way anybody around here gets that much cash.

"It has to be drug money," she says as Ti Jean and Will stuff the bundles into their backpacks. "The sheriff must be involved with the cartels."

Jack grins. "This just gets better and better."

"No, it doesn't," she says. "Put it back. Nobody screws around with the cartels. Don't you read the news?"

But Jack only continues to smile.

"Perhaps the good sheriff should have thought of that *before* he got into business with them," he says.

"Seriously," Maria says. "The cartels are too dangerous for us to mess around with."

"Don't worry," Jack tells her. "No one will be hurt—except, perhaps, for the sheriff, and he made this bed for himself."

He doesn't understand, Maria realizes. None of them do. They don't know how deadly the drug cartels are.

"Let's just leave," she tries again. "We should put the money back and leave right now."

"This money can help a lot of people," Jack says.

"I know. It's just…"

She doesn't want to lose him. She doesn't want him to be another casualty in the cartels' savage drug wars. That's what she wants to tell him. But she doesn't know how to say it without sounding clingy. She and Jack have only just met. They've only ever kissed so far.

The Glimmer Twins drift into the study while they're talking. One of them sprays "Liberated by Los Murrietas— all the sheriff's drug $$" on the wall beside the safe. The fresh paint looks like blood glistening on the white adobe surface. The other twin takes a picture of it with his phone. The flash is a momentary flare of light in the darkness.

Jack puts his finger under Maria's chin and looks into her eyes.

"Just what?" he asks, his voice soft.

Before she can answer he stiffens, head cocked as he listens for something Maria can't hear. But then she hears it, too. Tires on the pavement. On the street outside. Turning into the driveway.

"Everybody out, *now*," Jack says.

Maria is so scared she can barely join the scramble to get to the back door, but Jack keeps a steadying hand on her upper arm as he steers her toward the back patio.

"Stay together or split up?" Will asks as they run to the gate in the back fence.

"Together," Jack says.

He hands Maria off to Ti Jean and stops at the sheriff's koi pond. It's surrounded by a band of smooth loose pebbles the diameter of silver dollars. He grabs two handfuls and dumps them in his pockets, then hurries to catch up with the others.

"Don't worry," he tells Maria. "We'll be gone before the first cop car arrives at the front gates."

One of the Glimmer Twins is thumbing his phone as they make their way through the next yard.

"Posting your pictures?" Jack asks.

The twin nods and grins.

They keep going through the next yard, slipping from one into the next, darting across silent streets until they reach the outer wall of the community. Their rope is still hanging where they left it. One by one they shimmy up and over the wall. Maria listens for sirens, but the night is still quiet. She grabs the rope, but she's trembling so hard that she can't hold on to it.

Jack gives her a quick hug. "Trust me," he says before he climbs the rope to the top of the wall.

Ti Jean offers his hands to Maria as a stirrup, like he did with the Glimmer Twin on the way in. She steps into his laced fingers and up she goes like she's popping out of a jack-in-the-box. Jack catches her and swings her easily onto the ledge.

Ti Jean joins them, then quickly goes down the other side of the wall.

"Hang on until I let you go," Jack tells Maria as he takes hold of her wrists and eases her into a kneeling position, facing the community. Using the rampart to brace himself, he lowers her down the other side of wall, holding on until Ti Jean's strong hands on her hips lower her the rest of the way.

"I feel like such a wuss," she says as Jack makes his own nimble way down the rope.

"Don't," he tells her. "It's your first time. We've been doing this for ages."

She hugs herself. "I still can't figure out why there aren't any sirens."

"Maybe he didn't call his own officers," Will says. "Maybe he called his drug-running buddies instead."

Maria shivers. and Jack puts his arm around her shoulders.

"Let's get out of here," he says.

ONCE THEY get well away from El Rio Valley and there still aren't any sirens, Maria begins to relax.

Will takes out a list of people who need help that Luz made before she was arrested. The gang splits up, each taking some of the money, and although it's not even daybreak, they spend the next couple of hours delivering bundles of the stolen cash to those in need.

Maria is with Jack on the delivery run. Her spirits rise as they visit several homes on Calle Adelanto. At one house, they leave money to cover the expense of a child's asthma medicine. At another, the cash will keep a man from losing his burrito cart. At the third house, the old woman who answers the door ushers them inside with a smile that falters when she is offered money to pay her electricity bill.

She looks from Jack to Maria.

"Where did you get this money?" she asks. "Is it stolen?"

Maria knows many old women like this. The neighbourhood is full of them. Their brown skin is wrinkled, they move slowly and their once glossy dark hair is grey. They balance on the sharp edge of the poverty line, but they have their pride and are honest to a fault.

"We took it from a bad man, *señora*," Jack says. "You deserve it more than he does."

The woman shakes her head. "The devil has sent you. Do not tempt me."

Maria takes out the silver cross she wears on a chain under her dress.

"My friend is a good man," she says. She lifts the cross to her lips and kisses the silver. "I swear by Our Lady and *los santos*."

"Please, *señora*," Jack says. "Let us help you. We know you are alone in the world. Let us do what your children would if they were still here to look after you."

"My children...it was joining the gangs that killed them both."

"We have nothing to do with the bandas," Jack says. "We—"

His cell phone rings.

"*Pardon*," he says as he pulls it out of a pocket.

His eyes go dark as he listens to the voice on the other end.

"I'll be right there," he says before he cuts the connection.

"What is it?" Maria asks.

He shrugs. "Nothing, really. Just a little trouble—coincidentally, with the 66 Bandas. Will you wait for me here while I straighten it out?"

"But—"

"This is not the same as what we did earlier in the evening," he tells her. "That was like a game. In this, your inexperience will get you hurt."

"I'm not afraid."

"I know," he says. "But I'm afraid for you and I need all my wits about me. Don't worry. I won't be long."

He kisses her on the cheek, nods to the old woman, then slips out the door.

"I *knew* this had to do with gangs," the old woman says. "Everything bad in the barrio comes from their drugs and killing."

"We aren't with the gangs," Maria says. "We stand against them."

She can hardly believe the words coming out of her mouth. Before tonight, she would have been no different from the old woman standing in front of her. She would have believed that it was always better that the gangs didn't even know you existed.

But now she understands that ordinary people have to take matters into their own hands to help themselves. The police are corrupt and the government does nothing. The church can't keep up. And all the while, the rich hide behind the walls of their gated communities.

"Then you are doomed," the woman says. She makes the sign of the cross. "And you have brought them and their dirty money to my house."

"For that I apologize," Maria says.

Before the old woman can say any more, Maria opens the door and steps outside. She's surprised by the change in the light. The sun is rising above the Hierro Maderas. It's much brighter now than it was fifteen minutes earlier.

She remembers what Jack said about staying out of his way and slips through the old woman's dusty yard to the corner of the next house. Peering around its adobe wall she sees Jack and Ti Jean in the middle of the street. Jack's swinging something in one hand—she can't quite see what it is. A necklace perhaps. It's a blur, swinging too fast for her to see. Ti Jean is holding a length of saguaro rib as tall as he is.

Facing them are four men wearing the colours of the 66 Bandas. Coming down the street behind the bandas she sees Will approaching at a run. She can't spot either of the Glimmer Twins.

This is bad. Two of the bandas are carrying guns. The others have a machete and a tire iron. So far as she knows, her friends have no weapons—unless you could call Ti Jean's staff a weapon. But a saguaro rib is nothing against a gun or a machete, or even a tire iron.

Maria wants to hide her eyes, but she can't look away.

She looks around for something to use as a weapon. If the boys are going to fight, she will too.

But then she sees them. Three more bandas sneaking up through an alley behind Jack and Ti Jean. The buildings hide them from everyone except for her.

She cries out a warning to Jack.

In the alley, one of the bandas raises his gun. Maria feels the bullets punch into her chest before the sound of the gunshots register. They lift her up onto her toes and then she falls backwards, arms outspread. She hits the ground hard. She tries to suck in air but her lungs fill with blood.

She doesn't hear Jack's inarticulate cry. She doesn't see him spring into action.

The bottle tree man knew as soon as he saw Jack that the boy in the green hoodie was a marksman with any weapon—even it was only a stone in a sling. He would not be surprised by what happens next.

Jack had planned to only scare off the bandas. Break an arm, a leg. Incapacitate them.

Now, he shoots to kill.

He moves with supernatural speed, turns, looses a stone from his sling. Another. The bandas who shot Maria and the man beside him are dead before they even realize Jack has a weapon. Ti Jean charges the other four. Will comes at them from behind. The Glimmer Twins appear from a side yard and run to help.

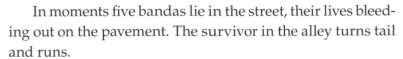

In moments five bandas lie in the street, their lives bleeding out on the pavement. The survivor in the alley turns tail and runs.

But for Maria, it is too late.

THE NEXT morning the news is full of the gang war between the 66 Bandas and Los Murrietas, which left seven dead on the barrio streets. There's also speculation about Sheriff Crase's involvement, fueled by his sudden disappearance and the photo the Glimmer Twins uploaded of the sheriff's safe with their message spray-painted on the wall above it.

No one pays attention to the release of Lucia Chaidez from county. With all the heat spilling over from the sheriff's office, the D.A. doesn't want to risk being seen as holding an innocent girl behind bars.

LUZ WALKS from the county jail to the camp the boys have outside of town. The camp's hidden under some cottonwoods where the San Juan River winds its dusty way along the back of a ranch on the east side of town. It's only during monsoons that water fills its banks.

Jack's not there.

"We haven't seen him since last night," Will says. "He walked out into the desert after we got back to camp and he hasn't come back."

Jack doesn't return until the funeral, three days later.

SANTA MARGARITA Maria church in the barrio is filled to capacity. The whole neighbourhood has heard that the bandas killed the leader of Los Murrietas, and everyone has come to the funeral service to pay their respects. Burly barrio boys without gang affiliations keep watch by the doors of the church and stand on street corners nearby in case the 66 Bandas are brazen enough to show up.

Luz sits unnoticed in a pew at the back where she hopes Pablo and the rest of Maria's family won't notice her. Jack and the boys are scattered through the congregation. Luz pays no attention to the crowd. She doesn't hear the priest. Her attention is on the photo of Maria on an easel beside the coffin.

Oh Maria, she thinks.

And she remembers.

Once upon a time, they were best friends.

EARLIER THIS year, when they are both nineteen, Luz comes back to Santo del Vado Viejo with Jack and the other boys. The first thing she plans to do is look up Maria.

"She's a good friend?" Will asks when she excitedly mentions this to the boys.

"She's my best friend."

"And here I thought I was your best friend," he says. He lays the back of his hand against his brow. "I'm so hurt."

She punches him in the shoulder and grins.

"Don't be silly," she tells him.

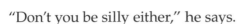

"Don't you be silly either," he says.

She's about to make another joke when she sees how serious he looks.

"What's up?" she says.

"What will you say when she asks what you're doing back in town? Will you invite her to join our little gang?"

"Of course not. I'm not going to tell her about any of that."

"But it will be hard keeping something so big from her."

She's about to say it's not even going to come up, but then she realizes how can it *not*? Maria will ask her lots of questions about her life. She'll ask if she found her magic. Luz will have to spin some story, but it won't do much good. Maria knows her too well. She'll see straight through any lie.

"It will be easier for both of you if you don't see her at all," Will says.

Ti Jean nods. "She doesn't sound like us. If she gets involved, she'll get hurt."

"If you love her," Jack says, "you'll let her go her own way."

The Glimmer Twins nod in agreement.

Though it upsets her, she knows they're right. She'll do what they say because the last thing she wants is for Maria to be hurt in any way.

"I really miss her. We were always best friends," she says.

"Then you have to decide," Jack says, "which is more important? The work, or her?"

She knows the answer to that, though she's not sure it's the right one because the decision is made by her head, not her heart.

But fate brings them together again anyway.

MARIA IS laid to rest in San Miguel Cemetery. Half
the barrio comes out to the graveyard, but Lucia is no
more aware of the crowd here than she was back in Santa
Margarita Maria. She watches as the coffin is lowered into
the ground. It feels like a piece of her is being buried with
Maria in that grave.

She stays long after the crowd is gone and the grave has
been filled in. She knows Jack and the boys are close by, but
they give her some distance.

Finally she hears a soft step in the dirt. Jack sits on his
haunches beside her.

"We were supposed to be together," Jack says. His tears
make tiny dark circles in the dirt at his feet.

"I didn't know until I saw her," he continues. "But as
soon as I did, I knew. She's my other half. We've only barely
met. How can it be that she's gone?"

Luz is wondering how any of this can be real. These
boys are spirits. Archetypes. *They* aren't real.

But Maria was. And Jack's sorrow is.

"I'm sorry," Luz says.

"That's not enough," Jack tells her.

He hands her the cigarette tin that Luz and Maria
magicked all those years ago.

"Bring her back," he says, his red-rimmed eyes pleading.

Luz accepts the tin, but all she can do is stare at it in her
hands, feeling helpless.

"I…I can't do that," she says. "I want to, but I wouldn't
even know how to begin."

"Look," Jack says. "I know who I am now. I'm the Jack in the Green—the Robin in the green hood. My companions and I have lived a hundred lifetimes in the green wood. In many ways we *are* the green wood. Yet your magics were still strong enough to bring us here, weren't they?"

She nods slowly. "But I didn't know what I was doing. I wasn't trying to bring you, specifically."

"The only reason you could bring us to you was because of *her*," Jack says. "Because she and I were destined to meet.

"I know how this charm works," Jack continues. "You think of Maria and you open the tin."

"And if nothing happens?"

"Something will happen," he assures her. "Every little thing we do makes something happen somewhere."

Luz looks at the tin. She remembers that night, rapping on Maria's window. She remembers the promise it held. She remembers how they took the tin to the bottle tree man's yard and buried it under the glass pebbles.

"Was it her magic or mine?" she asks, her voice soft.

"Does it matter? Open the tin."

She does and the world goes away.

Jack is ready this time. He catches Luz before she can fall over. He sits cross-legged and rests her head on his lap.

And like he did with Maria, he waits.

THE GREEN shocks Luz.

Jack and the boys are always talking about this ancient green wood of theirs, but she never thought it would be so verdant and lush.

She's used to cities like L.A., or the desert. Brown places with a horizon that lies in the far distance and a sky that stretches forever. Here, she can barely see the sky for the overhanging boughs of giant, mossy trees. The foliage has the wavy edges of oak leaves, but these are far bigger than any oak trees she's ever seen. The grass is thick underfoot. She would wonder about that—how it can grow so luxuriant and green with that thick canopy of leaves above—except she knows without having to be told that this place is like Jack, like the boys.

It's not a real wood, but the archetype of a wood.

She starts to walk. Her footsteps are almost silent on the grass, but the woods are full of birdsong. The air is moist, compared to the dry desert. It doesn't smell like dust. It smells like freshly turned earth and bark and leaves.

Luz should feel out of place. Her surroundings are unlike anything she's ever experienced before. Yet she feels like she's come home. And she's inexplicably happy.

She wanders aimlessly until she hears the sound of water. She follows the sound up a low incline until she comes to a spring-fed pool. Water tumbles from a cleft high in the rocks at its far end. Water lilies bloom on the surface of the pool and the rocks around it are covered in thick green moss. The giant oaks tower above, making it feel like a natural cathedral.

She's not surprised to find Maria sitting on one of those rocks, one hand trailing in the water. A shaft of light penetrates the trees, illuminating Maria's flawless brown skin and black hair. The white dress she's wearing glows in contrast to her surroundings. There are no holes in it, no blood. She looks like an angel.

Maria's gaze meets hers and she smiles, not in the least surprised to see Luz, either.

"You opened the tin," she says.

Luz nods. "Jack told me to."

Maria sighs. "Oh, Jack. All I ever got was a few kisses from him. But I feel like I've known him forever. We should have been together forever."

"He feels the same way."

Maria's eyes brighten, then she sighs again.

"Too bad I'm dead," she says.

"You're not—" Luz begins, except she doesn't really know what to say.

Maria *is* dead. She just watched her coffin being lowered into the dusty ground in San Miguel Cemetery.

"It's okay," Maria says. "You'd be surprised how quickly you get used to the idea. And this—" She waves her hand to take in their surroundings. "It's not such a bad place to be."

Neither of them says anything for a long moment.

"Jack seems to think he knew you from before," Luz says finally. "Like in some past life or something."

"That's so weird. But maybe it's true. I felt this immediate connection the first time I saw you guys robbing that house in Desert View. Maybe we did know each other, but I just can't remember. Or only my subconscious can."

"You could ask him," Luz says.

"Except I'm dead, so that's not really an option."

"I'm here to take you back," Luz tells her.

Maria's eyebrows go up. "Seriously? How does that work?"

"I'm not really sure."

"It's a nice thought," Maria tells her, "but I don't see it happening. Did you know they have talking foxes here?"

Luz shakes her head.

"They're so strange. They say I'm the maid of the green wood. That when the Summer King returns, he and I will... we'll make love, and that'll welcome in the spring. Our being together will make the year start or something." She shakes her head. "They call me Maid Marian instead of Maria, but I'm not their maid."

That makes Luz smile. And it fills her with the unexpected confidence that maybe this *can* be fixed.

"At home you *were* a maid," she says. "Just not the kind they expected. Come back, and you can be whatever you want to be."

"Come on. Remember me dying? I can't go back."

"There's always *brujería.*"

Maria shakes her head. "I don't think even magic can heal death. Luz, it's over. I felt each of those bullets as they tore through me." She plucks at the white cotton of her dress. "Even if they didn't leave any trace when I woke up here."

"Jack says if we're going to make things better we need to focus on that—the violence, not just the poverty."

"And how's he planning to fix that? Is he going to clean up the cartels?"

"We haven't figured it out yet," Luz says. "We need *you* to do that."

"Me? What do *I* know?"

"More than you think. But it's not just what you know. It's who you are. You're a martyr now. The woman the cartels and the bandas can't kill because she'll just come back. You can be the symbol of hope we need to stand against them."

"What if I don't want that? What if I just want to be an ordinary girl?"

"Oh Maria," Luz says. "You were never an ordinary girl."

"I still don't see how that brings me back."

"I think it's a matter of wanting to go back. You have to want it."

"If that's all it takes," Maria says, "pretty much everybody who ever died would go back."

"Maybe they do want to. But they don't have a magic cigarette tin like we do. When I was studying with Abuela she told me that magic depends mostly on our will. It's almost like, for it to work, you just have to believe that it will. Everything else—charms and spells and potions—those are just there to help us focus."

"Do *you* believe it?"

Luz breaks into a huge smile. " Oh, I *know* I'm going to bring you back," she says, holding out her hand.

Maria meets her gaze for a long moment before she stands up and takes Luz's hand. Their vision swims, the forest spins, and then the green is gone.

LUZ OPENS her eyes to find herself back in San Miguel Cemetery, lying with her head in Jack's lap. She grins up at him.

"I did it," she says, sitting up.

But then she sees that it's just her and the boys here at the graveside. Ti Jean offers her a hand and she lets him pull her to her feet. All her giddy good humour is gone. She turns to Jack.

"I thought...I was sure..." she begins, but her voice trails off.

She thinks she can still hear an echo of the birdsong from the green wood. She can almost feel the damp air. If she closes her eyes, she sees the green against the backs of her eyelids.

But the green wood is gone. She's back and Maria is still over there.

Maria is still dead.

ESPINOZA AMATE attended the funeral service at Santa Margarita Maria. It was there that she learned the full name of the young woman who died almost on her doorstep.

Maria Ana Martinez Reuda.

The newspapers had only referred to her as Maria Martinez, leader of Los Murrietas.

Espinoza doesn't agree with what the *banditos* were doing. Yes, they helped those in need, but it was with stolen money. Stealing is wrong, no matter what the excuse.

Espinoza still needs to pay her electric bill. The money the *banditos* left behind in her house she put in the collection box at Santa Margarita Maria. But she makes no judgment concerning the poor young woman. It isn't hers to make. Only God has the final word on such matters and Maria Ana Martinez Reuda is with Him now. It is to Him she must make her explanations.

Espinoza hopes the girl doesn't argue. She hopes she accepts that she has sinned. Only then will God forgive her.

After the service she lights a candle for the girl. She doesn't go out to the cemetery. It is too far to walk and she doesn't have the money for bus fare. She has always been frugal, but these days, especially, every penny counts.

Instead she goes back to her little house on Calle Adelanto and sits in a lawn chair on her front stoop. There she rests, rosary in hand, its beads moving through her fingers, her lips moving silently. She prays for the soul of Maria Ana Martinez Reuda.

Such a senseless death.

Espinoza prays for herself, as well. For forgiveness. She should never have let the girl go out into the dawn. She should have called her back, but fear stopped her. Fear of the 66 Bandas—what they would do if she interfered. And now because of her cowardice, the poor girl is dead.

The day is hot. There is dust in the air, as there always is in the barrio, and Espinoza is thirsty. She wishes she had lemons to make lemonade. She wishes—

Her mind goes still. She stands up and stares at the corner of her neighbour's house where the young girl died, her eyes widening with shock. She crosses herself.

The ghost of the dead girl has appeared there.

"*Madre de Dios.*"

Espinoza doesn't realize she spoke the words aloud until the dead girl turns in her direction.

"Hardly," Maria says. "I'm just me."

"Forgive me," Espinoza says. "I meant you no harm. Do not haunt me."

"I'm not haunting you."

Maria holds her hands up in front of herself and rubs them against each other.

"I'm just not dead anymore," she tells Espinoza.

"But that…that is impossible."

Maria smiles. "You'd think."

Espinoza only met the dead girl once when she was still alive, but that one meeting was enough for her to see the change in the girl now. Maria carries herself with an air of serenity and grace. In the old woman's eyes, she seems to glow from within.

Espinoza crosses herself again.

"You have become a saint," she says.

Maria shakes her head. "I think that's pretty unlikely. I'd need another couple of miracles under my belt first, and even then I don't think the church just hands sainthood to a barrio girl like me."

She crosses the dusty yard and comes up on Espinoza's stoop. She reaches out her hands. When Espinoza takes them she feels a tingle in her fingers that spreads through her whole body.

"You should sit," Maria says. "Rest a bit."

With the girl's help, Espinoza lowers herself back into her lawn chair.

"What will you do," Espinoza asks, "now that you have returned? Will you seek revenge on the bandas for killing you?"

Maria lets go of the old woman's hands.

"I don't know," she says. "Right now I just want to find my friends."

"They will be in…in the cemetery."

Maria nods. "I know."

Espinoza reaches for her, but Maria has already stepped back.

"Revenge is not the answer," she tells the girl. "Leave their judgment to God."

"Do you really think God pays any attention to people like you and me?"

"Of course I do."

Maria shakes her head. "I think maybe he expects us to help ourselves."

"Do not be swayed by dark desires, child. God has a plan for each one of us."

Maria smiles. "So who's to say whatever I do isn't his plan for me? *Vaya con Dios, señora.*"

Espinoza watches the girl walk across her lawn and down the street. She watches until she can't see her anymore, then she pushes herself up from her chair. She goes to her neighbour's house to tell her what she has seen.

Before the sun sets that evening, the whole barrio knows of the Miracle of Calle Adelanto.

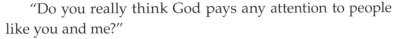

By midnight, a small shrine stands on the place where Maria died and then returned again. There are flowers and votive candles on the ground surrounding a white cross. Small milagros and folded scraps of paper holding prayers litter the ground.

Espinoza hides inside her house. Everyone wants to talk to her about her experience with the girl returned from the dead. Neighbours and strangers. Reporters. It's too much for the old woman and she wishes she'd never talked to anyone about it in the first place.

MARIA HAS every intention of going straight to San Miguel Cemetery, but as she continues down Calle Adelanto toward Mission Street she passes by Luna Diablo. She has never been inside. No one who values their own skin does since the Devil's Moon is one of the main hangouts of the 66 Bandas.

She stops in front of the bar without knowing why.

Except that's not true.

She knows what she's thinking of doing, but it's so *loco*— so like nothing she'd ever do—that she could never explain it if anyone were to ask. But dying and coming back changes something in you. Or at least it has changed her.

She hasn't become fearless. Knowing that something tangible lies beyond death has only made the idea of living sweeter. She understands that the gift of the world and her place in it is precious.

But for the bandas, life is a cheap commodity—a coin easily spent. Once that made her afraid. Now it makes her angry.

She knows Jack and Luz and the others are mourning her in the cemetery. Pablo, her family, Connie and Veronica and her other friends will be mourning her, too. She wants nothing more than to be with them. To reassure them that she has returned.

Instead, she enters the bar.

It's noisy—even at this time of the afternoon—but everything goes still the moment she steps inside. There are at least a dozen bandas seated at the various tables wearing their colours, and twice that number of hangers-on and girlfriends.

Sitting like a king at a center table is Roberto Pena, La Mano Grande. She knows him. Everybody knows him, if only to turn down another street when they see him coming. Today she walks right up to his table.

La Mano Grande doesn't have disproportionately big hands. He gets his nickname because when it comes to the barrio, he has his hand in everything illegal that can make money. Drugs, cars, guns.

He has tattoos on every visible piece of skin—even on his shaved head. It makes him seem like some kind of strange art installation—though he is far more dangerous than anything you might find in a gallery.

His gaze lingers on her as it travels up her body.

"I don't know who you are, *chica*," he finally says, "but unless you're offering up your sweets, you just stepped into a world of trouble."

He might not recognize her, but she sees that others in the room do. Eyes widen. More than one person makes the sign of the cross. The man sitting beside Pena picks a newspaper up from the floor and drops it on the table in front of the gang leader. Pena glances down at it.

"So what?" he asks. "You her sister or something?"

"Tell yourself that, if it makes you feel better, but it doesn't change who I am."

"You don't look like a ghost to me."

"I'm not," Maria says. "I just came back."

He gives her a smile that doesn't reach his eyes.

"Is that supposed to scare me?" he says. "You don't scare me. I could have you killed just like that."

He snaps his fingers.

Maria doesn't start. A strange calm has fallen over her. Her gaze is steady as it meets his. He reaches behind his back and pulls a handgun from his belt. He lays it on the table, his hand resting beside it.

"Go ahead," she tells him. "But the next time I return from the dead I won't come with the same courtesy as today. The next time I might come to your bedside, and you could die without ever knowing I was there."

She can see that she's getting to him. He knows she's not afraid in the same way the barrio dogs can smell fear. It makes him cautious. He didn't become the leader of the 66 Bandas because he's stupid. He became the leader because he's acutely perceptive and considers all possibilities before he acts.

"Is there a point to this?" he asks.

Maria nods. "Keep your business out of the barrio. I'm tired of seeing old ladies scared to leave their houses because your macho men are strutting around. I'm tired of innocent people dying in drive-bys. I'm tired of this place being a war zone, twenty-four/seven. You know, even wild animals don't shit in their own nests."

Pena continues to hold her gaze. He tries to give nothing away.

"I thought you people just robbed rich gringos," he says. "Why are you messing with us?"

"Are you even listening to me?"

He shrugs. "You open your mouth and all I hear is blah-blah-blah."

She starts to turn to leave and Pena picks up the gun, pointing it at her.

"Did I say you could go?" he asks.

"Shoot me or don't," Maria says, "Either way, I'm going to catch the tail end of my graveside service."

"Yeah, yeah. Because you'll just come back and kill me in my sleep. But maybe I won't kill you. Maybe I'll just blow out your knees and your elbows and let you live for awhile."

Maria braces herself for the shots, but they don't come. After a long moment, Pena lays the gun down on the table again.

"The Garzas want their money back," he says.

"Who are the Garzas?"

"The Garza Cartel," he says like he's talking to an idiot.

"And I told you what I want," Maria says.

"Nobody cares what you want. I'm letting you walk out of here in one piece so that you can bring me the money you stole from Crase. You've got twenty-four hours."

"And if I don't come back?"

"Don't make me send my boys out looking for you," Pena tells her. Maria waits to see if he has anything to add. Finally she turns around and starts for the door again. She expects a bullet in the back at any moment.

"And, *chica*," Pena calls after her.

She stops, but doesn't turn her head in his direction.

"I'll shit wherever I want—¿tú entiendes?"

Maria leaves without acknowledging him.

She welcomes the sun on her face when she steps outside. A shiver starts up in the pit of her stomach and goes through her entire body.

Up close to La Mano Grande as she'd been, she'd seen the edge of crazy in his eyes. But was she any less *loco* than Pena, she wonders to herself.

What had she hoped to accomplish in there, anyway?

She realizes she has no idea, and continues down Calle Adelanto to Mission Street.

Maybe she just wanted to look into the face of the enemy before she helped bring him down.

MARIA IS filled with anxiety when the bus stops at San Miguel Cemetery. She thinks she'd rather be walking back into Luna Diablo than face what is to come. She feels so guilty for what she put her family and friends through. Mamá and Papá will be devastated. Pablo will be so angry. Connie and Veronica...

Who else will be there?

How can she even begin to explain being back?

But when she walks through the gates she sees only Luz, Jack and the boys standing around a mound of fresh earth, heads bowed. Will is the first to notice her. He gives a shout and then they're all running towards her, grinning. As Jack's gaze meets hers her panic ebbs, replaced by a sudden shyness. But he gives her no chance to be reticent. He catches her up in his arms and lifts her, turning in a circle, holding her close.

Maria responds gladly. The shyness goes the way of the panic and she's glad to be back with them all again. Their voices are a babble of happy sounds all around her, everybody taking their turn to give her a hug.

For the first time since she came back she feels real. She looks at Luz, who is grinning from ear to ear.

It takes awhile for everything to calm down. Then Maria asks the question that has been lying under her happiness to trouble her:

"Where is everyone else? Did only you come?"

Will smiles. "Oh, girl. You should have seen it. The church was packed from front to back, and half the barrio came to the cemetery for the service here. Who knows how many people will show up at the community center for the potluck?"

"Your funeral was awesome," one of the Glimmer Twins agrees.

"And my parents...my family..."

"They were all here," Luz says. "They're really broken up."

Maria nods. "I have to go see them—to let them know I'm...you know..."

"Not dead," Ti Jean says.

Maria nods again.

"It's weird that you didn't come back when I did," Luz says.

"Maybe I did," Maria says. "When you took my hand everything spun away and I found myself back where I died."

Jack gives her shoulders a sympathetic squeeze.

"That must have been hard," he says.

"No, it was okay," she says. "But then I did something stupid."

She tells them about the old woman seeing her appear where she'd died, and how she went into Luna Diablo to confront La Mano Grande. They're all quiet when she's done. She's grateful that no one points out how crazy she was to go there.

"Twenty-four hours," Will finally says. "That's not a lot of time."

Jack nods. "But doable. And now we know whose money it was." He smiles at Maria. "You go to the community center. See your family. We'll deal with this."

"Deal with it?" she says. "This isn't just robbing some house. This is the cartels. You're just five guys."

"Yeah," Ti Jean says with a wink, "but we're mythic, so we'll be okay."

"It's not a joke," Maria starts, but Luz lays a hand on her arm.

"I'll go with you to see your family," she says.

"But…"

"Let the boys handle it."

"TWENTY-FOUR HOURS," Ti Jean says as they watch the girls leave the cemetery. "The bandas aren't going to wait any twenty-four hours."

Jack nods. "I know. They're giving her just long enough to go to her family. Then they'll hit the whole place and have a room full of hostages to make sure they get their money."

None of the boys speak. They all know that the money is gone, already given away to those in need. There's no time to steal that much again in time to save Maria and the funeral mourners.

Her miraculous return is about to turn from joy to horror. Maria and Luz will die. All her friends and family will die. The cartels make a point of sending clear messages about anyone who crosses them.

"So what do we do?" Will finally asks.

Jack turns to him. "We stop them."

"We have to get this Mano Grande," one of the Glimmer Twins says.

"Yeah," the other twin adds. "He already killed her once."

Jack's eyes are dark with anger.

"Oh, I remember," he says. "He's first on my list."

"We're going to need an army," Will says.

"I know," Jack says. "We'll have to call in the rest of the boys."

His companions exchange glances.

"But," Ti Jean begins.

Jack holds up his hand.

"Don't say it. I know what it means," Jack tells him. "If we do this, we have to go back to the green wood. Maria will be safe, but we won't see her again."

He looks around at them, meeting their gazes one by one. "I can't ask you to do this for me."

Will laughs. "You're kidding, right?"

Jack doesn't smile. He lays a fist against his chest.

"You honour me with your loyalty," he says.

The boys respond with the same gesture.

"Okay," Ti Jean says. "Let's get this show on the road."

Jack nods. "The Glimmer Twins will go back to camp to get our weapons. We'll meet you at the community center."

IT WAS so hard to go to the cemetery. But this is harder still. Maria knows she would not be able to do this without Luz at her side.

The community center is full of people when they step through the door, arm in arm. Her cousin Rico is first to notice. His eyes widen and he makes the sign of the cross. Beside him, an older man is the next to see her. He clutches the table and has to be lowered into his chair. Maria recognizes him. It's Juan Valdez, the undertaker. He lives just down the street from her parents' house. Of course they would go to him.

A ripple of silence spreads from Rico and Señor Valdez through the hall until it reaches the table at the far side of the room where her parents are sitting. For a long moment, all they can do is stare. Then Mamá stands slowly and approaches the two girls, leaning on Pablo for support. Pablo's face is white. Papá walks on the other side of him.

But before her family can reach her, Maria hears a high-pitched squeal. She turns to see Connie and Veronica running towards her.

Luz drops her arm and steps aside.

"Oh my God, oh my God!" Connie cries.

Then her girls are on Maria, firing questions, hugging her, crying. Veronica's eye make-up runs. They only step back when her family has come close.

"Maria Ana?" Mamá says.

She looks so old, Maria thinks. Both her parents do. This has been harder on them than it has been on her.

She steps toward her mother, arms outstretched. Mamá clutches both her hands. She pulls Maria in close and begins to weep. Papá puts a tentative hand on her shoulder, as though he's assuring himself that his returned daughter is flesh and blood, not a ghost. Then he holds both her and Mamá in a tight embrace.

The silence is the room is so profound that Maria can hear the pulse of her own blood.

Mamá pulls away, but still holds on with one hand. She wipes her tears with the other.

"Sis?" Pablo says. "How—how is this possible?"

"I don't know," she tells him. "I remember dying, but then I was back, standing in the same place I fell. It was like I'd never been hurt. I didn't even know what had happened until an old woman told me about the funeral."

"The things I have heard," Mamá says. She shakes her head. "They think you're a part of that gang—the one that robs all the rich people."

"Los Murrietas," Maria says.

Mamá nods. "Such nonsense. I have told the reporters a thousand times that you have nothing to do with them."

Maria's gaze goes to Luz, who gives a small shake of her head. But Maria knows why she was allowed to come back.

"That's not true," she says. "I was their leader."

Her mother sways and has to lean on Papá. She makes the sign of the cross. The crowd in the community center presses closer to hear.

"This is *loco*," Mamá says.

Maria shakes her head. "No, it's about justice. Here in the barrio we are stuck between the banks and the bandas, and there is nothing left over for the rest of us. If no one will help us, we have to help each other."

Mamá is shaking her head the whole time Maria is talking.

"No, no," she says. "You will come to harm. You have already come to harm."

"I know it's dangerous," Maria says. "But I came back, didn't I?"

She looks to her father and brother, but she can't tell what they're thinking. Before she can ask, a gunshot booms in the parking lot outside the building and the quiet murmur of conversation that had been building up in the community center is cut off again.

"Where's my little Maria?" a familiar voice calls from outside. "Or better yet, where's my money?"

Luz clutches Maria's arm.

"Is that who I think it is?" she says.

Maria nods. "La Mano Grande."

"What's he doing here? Didn't you say he gave you twenty-four hours?"

"I guess he lied."

The guests in the community center all move away from the door. They gather on the sides of the room, leaving only the two girls and Maria's family in the open space in front of the door. A buzz of whispered conversation starts up again, with many worried looks to the entrance.

Maria kisses her mother, then her father and brother.

"What are you doing?" Mamá says as Maria turns to walk to the door.

"Maria, this isn't your fight anymore," Luz says.

Connie grabs Maria's arm.

"Yeah, don't be crazy here," Veronica says.

But Maria pulls gently away. She knows what she must do. This is why she was allowed to come back. The bandas were always going to come after their money. Somehow, she will stop this from getting any worse than it already is. She will gladly die again if it means the violence will spare her family and friends.

Mamá puts her hand on her shoulder, but Maria lifts it and kisses it before letting it drop.

"Don't be sad, Mamá," Maria says. "This was just my chance to say a proper goodbye. Think of it as a gift from the saints."

Kissing her cheek again, Maria walks to the door. Papá puts his arm around Mamá. Maria's brother and her girls stand by the pair, watching Maria go.

"Stay with my family," she says when Luz falls in step beside her.

"Like hell I will," Luz tells her.

Maria doesn't try to talk her out of it. Nobody ever won an argument with Luz.

La Mano Grande gives them a big grin when they step outside. A revolver dangles from his hand, pointed at the ground. Behind him, ranged across the parking lot, are almost two dozen men all wearing the colours of the 66 Bandas.

"There you are, my little *bandita*," he says. "Now where's my money?"

"You said I had twenty-four hours."

Pena shrugs. "I'm an impatient man."

"No," a voice says from the side of the building. "You are a dishonourable man."

Maria has a moment of hope as she hears Jack speak, but when she turns in his direction she sees he stands there alone in his green hoodie, with nothing more than a long-bow in his hands. He has an arrow notched and the string is slack. It will take him just a moment to draw and shoot. But it's only an arrow. Pena's men are many and they're armed with guns.

"Who the hell are you?" Pena demands.

"A man who keeps his word," Jack says. "And I promise you this: threaten my friend again, and you and all your men will die here today."

Pena laughs. "Do you hear this?" he asks his men. "He's going to shoot us all with one arrow."

The bandas laugh. Pena starts to lift his gun.

"I wouldn't do that," Jack says.

"Why not?" Pena asks. "You think you can shoot faster?"

His men are still laughing, but they are lifting their weapons as well. When Pena almost has his gun raised, Jack draws the bowstring back and shoots so fast that Maria doesn't even see him do it. The arrow drives straight through Pena's left kneecap and he falls to the ground, his gun tumbling from his hand onto the dirt.

Now they'll kill us all, Maria thinks.

But at the same time that Jack shoots, a rain of arrows falls upon the bandas. Maria looks up and sees that every rooftop facing the parking lot has almost a dozen archers on it, all of them dressed in green.

"You piece of shit!" Pena yells.

He crawls for his gun and Jack shoots him again, this time shattering the elbow of the arm reaching for the weapon. Maria hears the bones splinter.

"Now, what was it you said you'd do to Maria?" Jack asks.

He walks toward the fallen gang leader, drawing another arrow from the quiver hanging from his shoulder.

"Oh, yes," he says. "I remember what she told me."

He fires again, piercing Pena's other knee.

"You were going to shoot out her knees and elbows."

"You're a dead man, *puto.*"

"Look around you," Jack says. "It's your men who are dead."

His voice is conversational, but Maria shivers at the steel in it. She's uncomfortable with Jack's

casual cruelty until she thinks of what the bandas would have done to her family and friends. What they have already done to the people of this neighbourhood. They're like the bankers, always walking around like kings. The only difference is, the bankers would never come to this neighbourhood in the first place. And the bandas aren't remotely subtle in how they treat other people like dirt.

Pena manages to push himself upright on one arm to look around the parking lot. All his men are down. Most are dead. Those who aren't are too incapacitated to be of any help. Archers line the rooftops with drawn bows—more than he can count. More men in green hoods come down every side street.

"Where the hell did he get all those guys?" Luz says.

But Maria knows. She only has to look at them to smell the deep forest they carry inside them. There's a piece of it inside her, as well.

"They're the foxes," she says. "The ones from the green wood."

Luz's mouth shapes a soundless "O."

"This is nothing," Pena says turning back to Jack. "You think you've got balls? My bosses are going to level this place when they find out what you've done. They'll hunt you down and stake you out in the desert."

"You're kidding, right?" Jack says. "The cartels are businessmen. There's no percentage in avenging a bunch of losers. They'll just find some other gang to work for them."

For a long moment Pena glares at him. Then he spits in the dirt.

"Go ahead," he says. "Kill me. I'm not afraid to die."

Jack shakes his head. "I only said I'd kill you if you threatened my friend again."

He draws his bow and shoots again. This arrow rips through Pena's other elbow. Pena collapses, head banging on the packed dirt.

"Now, if you're lucky," Jack says, "one of the good people here in the neighbourhood will call you an ambulance. I mean, they've got to have some love and respect for you, right?"

He turns away to face Maria. She watches the hardness leave his features. The eyes that promised her everything when their gazes first met are filled with sorrow.

"I can't stay," he says. "By calling my men here I've forfeited my right to remain."

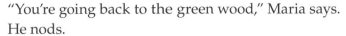

"You're going back to the green wood," Maria says.

He nods.

"Then I'm coming with you," she tells him.

"No," he says. "You have a second chance at life here."

"I don't want a second chance here. I want to be with you." She pauses, then adds, "Unless you don't want to be with me."

He answers by taking her in his arms and giving her a long kiss.

"Jeez, get a room, people," Luz says.

They step apart, still holding hands.

"You're going right now?" Luz asks.

Maria looks to Jack. He nods.

"Are you going to say goodbye to your parents?"

Maria shakes her head. "They already said their goodbyes to me in the church and cemetery. It's better if they think they only saw a ghost today."

Luz sighs. "I wish I could go with you."

Maria shakes her head. "You can't. You still have work to do. A life to live."

"What if I open the cigarette tin again? Maybe I'll be able to come to visit."

"Maybe."

Maria smiles, but she presses closer to Jack—so close there is no separation between their bodies.

"But don't try it for at least a few days," she says with a wink.

A wind picks up out of nowhere, swirling dust around the parking lot. When it clears, Maria and the men in their green hoods are all gone. Only the bandas are there now, the wounded and the dead.

People from the neighbourhood venture out into the parking lot. Some of them stand around La Mano Grande. He offers them money—anything they want—if they will phone for help before he bleeds out. No one takes him up on his offer.

Luz puts a hand in her pocket and wraps her fingers around the small cigarette tin. It's all she has left of Maria.

Once upon a time, they were best friends.